This book belongs to:

_____

_____

_____

To my daughter, Anna,

Who wanted a unicorn with a tutu!

Today I overheard my friend say,

NEVER LET A UNICORN WEAR A TUTU!

Unfortunately, I didn't have a chance to ask why.

Now I have this fantastic tutu for my UNICORN,

and I'm not sure what to do!

This TUTU was specifically made

FOR A UNICORN!

It says so on the tag! So... what could go wrong?

UNICORN immediately tried it on!

First, SHE DANCED!

Next, SHE TWIRLED!

After that, SHE PRANCED!

It was great to see her so HAPPY!

Then, she did something that I wasn't expecting...

She took off running!

WHERE ARE YOU GOING!?!

I shouted!

I soon found her at my shoe rack!
Apparently, a TUTU needs to be
accessorized with shoes...

I calmly explained to UNICORN that this will be the ONLY TIME she can borrow my boots!

After I got the boots on UNICORN, she wanted
me to wear some fancy boots, too...

At first I was reluctant, but I finally agreed.

But then she took off running...

AGAIN!!!

This time
she got into
my BOWS!!!

STOP!!!

I yelled.

After UNICORN put bows in her mane and tail, she wanted me to wear bows, too! And once again, she took off running!

WHERE ARE YOU GOING NOW?!?

I hollered.

NO!!!
NOT THE JEWELRY!!!
I screeched.

But it was too late.
Necklaces, rings, and bracelets
were flying everywhere!

After UNICORN layered herself in
jewelry, she wanted me to wear jewelry, too...

But then she took off running... AGAIN!

UNICORN headed right for the kitchen and started tossing CUPCAKES at me!

Miraculously, all the cupcakes landed perfectly
on the plate! I thought UNICORN would be ecstatic,

I HAD SAVED ALL THE CUPCAKES!

But instead, a little tear drop ran down her cheek.

She looked so upset...

I tried to figure out what had happened,
but I couldn't understand what
UNICORN was trying to say.

I started to think, if I were a unicorn, with an amazing tutu, fancy boots, sparkling bows, dazzling jewelry, and yummy cupcakes...

WHY WOULD I BE SAD?

I soon realized that there was one thing missing...

I quickly rushed to my closet...

I began rummaging through my clothes and I pulled out a
TUTU
and announced...
TWINSIES!

UNICORN jumped for joy!

UNICORN made me feel special all day!
She included me from the minute she tried on
the TUTU, the fancy boots, the hair bows, and the dazzling
jewelry. She even invited me to eat the yummy cupcakes!

It all makes sense now...

NEVER LET A UNICORN WEAR A TUTU

unless...

YOU'RE WEARING A MATCHING ONE, TOO!

The End.